Puffin Books

DODIE

Dodie is a very clever little dachshund dog, with a talent for finding things. This is very lucky, because Miss Smith is always losing things. In these four delightful stories, Dodie finds Tigercat's missing kitten and a prickly hedgehog.

Finola Akister lives in Aylesbury, Bucks, and has worked as a cartographical draughtswoman. Her first book was a collection of poems entitled *Before You Grow Up*.

Also by Finola Akister

BEFORE YOU GROW UP

Finola Akister

Dodie

Illustrated by Barbara Walker

PUFFIN BOOKS

PUFFIN BOOKS

Published by the Penguin Group
27 Wrights Lane, London W8 5TZ, England
Viking Penguin Inc., 40 West 23rd Street, New York, New York 10010, USA
Penguin Books Australia Ltd, Ringwood, Victoria, Australia
Penguin Books Canada Ltd, 2801 John Street, Markham, Ontario, Canada L3R 1B4
Penguin Books (NZ) Ltd, 182–190 Wairau Road, Auckland 10, New Zealand

Penguin Books Ltd, Registered Offices: Harmondsworth, Middlesex, England

First published by Viking Kestrel 1989
Published in Puffin Books 1990
10 9 8 7 6 5 4 3 2 1

Made and printed in Great Britain by
Richard Clay Ltd, Bungay, Suffolk
Filmset in Times (Linotron 202)

Contents

Dodie and the Lost Key

Dodie was a dachshund dog. He had great big brown eyes and floppy ears. He had a long thin body and very, very short legs.

It made him look a bit like a walking sausage.

7

Dodie lived in a country cottage with an old lady who was called Miss Smith.

Miss Smith also had a cat called Tigercat. It was covered all over in stripes, just like a real tiger.

Miss Smith was always
forgetting where she put things.
She would forget where she had
put her slippers. She would

forget where she had left the daily paper, and even where she had left her knitting.

Dodie was good at finding things. He would run and fetch the slippers or anything else that Miss Smith could not find. Then Miss Smith would say, "Oh, Dodie, what a clever little dog you are. Whatever would I do without you?"

Dodie and Tigercat were very good friends. Tigercat allowed Dodie to use her little cat-flap.

It was a very useful cat-flap because it saved Miss Smith having to get up to let either Dodie or Tigercat go out into the garden. Or to let them come in from the garden.

One day Miss Smith set off to
go to the shop. She put on her
hat and coat and off she went,
down the garden path and out
into the road.

Dodie had just settled down to have a sleep when he heard a rat-tat-tat on the door. Then he heard Miss Smith calling to him.

"Dodie, can you hear me? I've forgotten my key and locked myself out of the house. Do you think you could find it?"

Dodie was puzzled. What was a key? Miss Smith had never asked him to find a key before. He had no idea what a key looked like. How could he find something he didn't know about?

He went and woke up Tigercat. Perhaps she would know what a key looked like.

Tigercat stretched lazily and opened one eye.

"Do you know anything about a thing called a key?" asked Dodie.

"Don't bother me," miaowed Tigercat. "Of course I don't know anything about a key. Cats aren't supposed to know about things like that." She closed her eye and went back to sleep.

Dodie thought very hard. Perhaps if he found all the usual things that Miss Smith asked for, the key might be among them.

First he picked up the paper and pushed it out through the cat-flap. "No, Dodie, not the paper. Do try and find the key," said Miss Smith.

Then Dodie pushed her knitting through the cat-flap. After that he pushed all sorts of things through it. There was the

tea-cosy, Miss Smith's library book, her woolly cardigan and even the dustpan and brush.

As Dodie pushed more and more things through the cat-flap, Miss Smith grew very

worried. "Oh dear," she said, "if Dodie keeps pushing out things I will soon have everything that ought to be in the house out here in the garden."

She tried once more. "Dodie, my dear, all I want is the key to unlock the door. Do try and find it."

Inside the house Dodie looked about him. He had pushed all the things Miss Smith normally asked him to find through the cat-flap. None of them was what she wanted. The only other thing he could see was the bag thing that she usually took shopping with her. She called it her handbag.

Taking hold of the bag by the strap, Dodie dragged it along the hallway and pushed it out through the cat-flap.

"At last," cried Miss Smith. "Oh, Dodie, whatever would I do without you? You are a clever little dog."

She opened her handbag and there inside was the key. Taking it out, she unlocked the door and was soon safely inside the cottage.

Miss Smith was so upset by being locked out of her cottage that she decided to make herself a cup of tea. But where was the tea-cosy?

"Dodie, have you any idea where I have left the tea-cosy?" she asked.

Poor Dodie; he knew exactly where the tea-cosy was. It was outside in the garden with all the other things that he had pushed through the cat-flap.

Sighing a doggy sort of sigh, Dodie went out through the cat-flap and started to push back into the cottage all the things he had pushed outside into the garden.

Before he had finished,
Matthew, the boy who lived
next door, came to take Dodie
for a walk. He was so surprised
to see all the things in the
garden.

Matthew helped Dodie to take them all back into the cottage. Then he and Dodie went for a walk in the park.

Dodie and the Snowy Day

One morning Dodie looked out of the window. What a surprise he got. Everything was white. The grass was white, the trees were white. Even the garden gate was white.

"Look, Tigercat," he woofed,
"the whole world has turned
white."

Tigercat got out of her basket
and gave a big yawn. Then she
went and looked out of the
window.

"Oh, it's been snowing," she
told Dodie. "It did that once
before, I remember. All that

white stuff is very cold and very wet."

Then Tigercat went back to her basket and promptly went to sleep again.

Dodie was too excited to even think of going back to bed. He had never seen snow before and he wanted to go out and play in it.

Off he went down the hall and through the cat-flap.

As soon as his paws touched the snow he could feel how cold it was but he didn't care. He ran down the path, across the lawn and back again. Everywhere he went he left four little footprints behind him in the snow.

What fun it was. Dodie ran round and round in circles just to see how many footprints he could make. Soon the garden was full of footprints.

Next he tried to eat some. That was fun too. It tasted just like water but it was very much colder.

Dodie was having such a
lovely time when he heard Miss
Smith calling to him. "Dodie,
you're getting so wet, you had
better come in now."

Dodie didn't mind getting all wet. He was having far too much fun. However, he thought that Miss Smith might want him to find something for her, so he had better go in.

Miss Smith didn't like the snow. She was frightened that if she went out in it she might fall and hurt herself.

Dodie gave a big doggy sigh. It looked as though he would have to go without his walk.

There was a knock on the
door and when Miss Smith

answered it, there stood Matthew and his brother, Jonathan. "Hello, Miss Smith," said Matthew, "we've come to see if there is anything you want from the shop. Mum says you might not like to go out in all this snow."

"Your mother is quite right," answered Miss Smith. "I'm so afraid that I might fall. Perhaps you would get me a white sliced loaf and a pound of carrots at the shop."

"Of course we will," answered Jonathan. "Do you think Dodie would like to come for a walk?"

Dodie wagged his tail to show just how much he wanted to go for a walk in all the lovely snow. Then, just to make certain that Miss Smith would understand, he ran and fetched his lead.

When Miss Smith and the boys saw him standing there with the lead in his mouth, they all laughed.

It didn't take them long to get
to the shop and buy the bread
and carrots for Miss Smith.
"Shall we go to the playground
and see what it's like covered in
snow?" asked Matthew. "I bet
Dodie would like that,"
answered Jonathan.

When they got to the playground they let Dodie off his lead so that he could have a scamper in the snow. There were other children there who were very busy building a snowman. Matthew and Jonathan joined in the fun.

Soon they had made a lovely big snowman. "That looks quite

good," said a girl called Jenny, "but it ought to have some eyes and a nose."

All the children looked in their pockets to see if they could

find anything that would do for the snowman's eyes and nose.

One boy who was called Tommy had some big marbles. "These will do for his eyes," he said. When he put them in the snowman's face they looked just like real eyes.

Matthew thought about the carrots he had just bought for Miss Smith. He couldn't help thinking what a lovely nose one of them might make. He also wondered if Miss Smith would mind too much if he used one of them to make the snowman a nose.

He asked Jonathan. "Oh,

Miss Smith would be glad to give the snowman a nose," said Jonathan. Then Matthew took a carrot out of the bag and put it in the snowman's face.

Jenny looked at the snowman. "His nose is too long," she said. "It makes him

look too beaky." She took the
carrot out of the snowman's face
and broke it in half. Then she
put just half the carrot back in
the snowman's face. It was
much better.

All the children were so
pleased with their snowman.

"Let's go and see if the pond is frozen," suggested Tommy. It sounded like a good idea so they all ran off towards the pond.

The pond was frozen. All the ducks stood around, looking very unhappy. They could not swim in the water and they were all unhappy because there was nothing to eat and they were all hungry.

Jenny was very sorry for them. She turned to Matthew. "Do you think Miss Smith would mind if we gave them just

one slice of her bread?" she asked.

"I don't know," answered Matthew. "We've already used one of her carrots for the snowman."

"The ducks do look very hungry," pleaded Jenny. "Just one slice?"

They took a slice of bread and broke it into tiny pieces. Then they threw them to the ducks.

There were so many ducks that some of them didn't get a single piece of bread. Then Matthew took another slice of bread and gave that to the ducks.

By the time all the ducks had had some bread there was only half of the loaf left.

When the children got back to the cottage, they were frightened that Miss Smith

would be very cross. Miss Smith
only laughed and said, "Half a
loaf is better than none, and I'm
sure that your snowman looks
very smart with his carrot
nose."

They were all so glad that
Miss Smith wasn't cross.

As for Dodie, he'd had so much fun running around in the snow. He was so happy and so tired that he stretched out in front of the fire and was soon fast asleep.

Dodie and the Lost Kitten

Dodie was woken up very early one morning by some very odd, squeaky noises. They were coming from Tigercat's basket.

There were the usual purring noises that Tigercat made when

she was happy. Dodie was used to that. These squeaky noises puzzled him.

It sounded as though something needed oiling, but as Dodie couldn't think what it could be that needed oiling, he decided to go over and look in Tigercat's basket.

Tigercat was lying in her
basket and snuggled up to her
were lots of fluffy little kittens.

"Hello, Dodie," purred
Tigercat. "What do you think of
my babies?"

Dodie was so surprised that
he could only stand and stare.
Then he started to count. One,

two, three, four, five.

"They are lovely," said
Dodie. "What a lot of babies to
have all at once. They're all
covered in stripes, just like
you."

Dodie ran upstairs to tell Miss
Smith about Tigercat's babies.

Miss Smith was fast asleep
because it was very early in the
morning. When she heard

Dodie barking, she woke up with a start. "Whatever is the matter?" she asked. Then she followed Dodie downstairs.

She was so surprised to see Tigercat's kittens. "What a clever puss you are," she said as she stroked Tigercat.

Miss Smith started to count the kittens. One, two, three, four, five and six.

Six, thought Dodie. He had only counted five. He poked his nose into Tigercat's basket and started to count all over again. It wasn't easy to count them because they kept moving about.

Then Dodie got another surprise. There was another kitten but it wasn't covered in stripes. It was all black.

"Good grief," exclaimed Dodie. "There are six kittens. Five stripy ones and a black one."

"Well, we'll certainly have to call that one Blackie," said Miss Smith. Then she sat down and started to think what names she would call the others.

Soon the kittens were big enough to crawl all over the floor. Tigercat was kept very busy trying to make sure that they didn't scamper too far from the cat basket.

One day, Tigercat was very
worried. She asked Dodie if he
had any idea where Blackie
might be. She had looked in all
the nooks and crannies in the
kitchen and she could not find
him anywhere.

"I will help you find him, he
can't be far away," said Dodie.
They searched everywhere in
the kitchen. They looked high
and low, up and down, in and
out, but there was no sign of the
missing kitten.

Miss Smith joined in the search. She looked under the sink, she looked under the cooker. There was no sign of Blackie.

She even started to look in
the most unlikely places. She
looked in the bread-bin, inside
the cupboards, and even inside
the rubbish bin. There wasn't
the least sign of the missing
kitten.

They were still searching
when Matthew and Jonathan
called to take Dodie for a walk.
When they heard about the
missing kitten they too joined in
the search.

Soon Jenny and Tommy
called and they also joined in
the search.

Then the milkman came.
When he heard that Blackie was
lost he also joined in the search.

The postman came and
started to look for Blackie.

The little cottage was full of
people all searching for Blackie.
They could not find him.

"Wherever can he be?" said
Miss Smith. She was getting
very worried.

Then Dodie had an idea. He knew that he wasn't a bloodhound type of dog; the sort that sniffed out things. Still, he was a dog. He would try to sniff out Blackie.

First he sniffed at Tigercat's basket. Yes, it was full of scents to follow. He would follow one. He sniffed across the kitchen floor, then he sniffed along the hall. The scent led him to the

umbrella stand near the front door.

There were Miss Smith's walking shoes and tucked up in one of them was Blackie. He was fast asleep.

"Woof, woof," barked Dodie. He wanted to tell everyone that he had found the missing kitten.

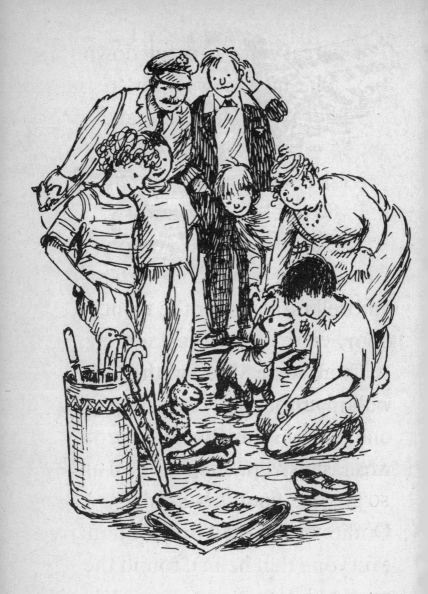

Tigercat came running down the hall. She was so happy to have her kitten back safe and sound.

Miss Smith came down the hall. So did Matthew and Jonathan, Jenny and Tommy. Then the milkman followed by the postman.

When they saw Blackie they were all so pleased that he had been found.

"What a clever little dog you are," said Miss Smith. "You are so good at finding things. Whatever would we do without you?"

Dodie was very pleased to have found Blackie, but most of all he was happy because it was time for him to go for a walk with the children.

Dodie and the Nervous Hedgehog

It was such a nice hot sunny day. Dodie was lying on the lawn and dreaming about lovely things like bones, doggy dinners and going for walks.

Suddenly he heard Miss Smith calling to him. "Dodie, Dodie, I've lost my garden trowel. Do you think you could find it for me?"

Dodie was very clever at finding all the things that Miss Smith lost. She would just put things down and forget where she had put them.

Usually Dodie knew exactly where Miss Smith had put things down but the garden trowel was different. No matter how hard he thought, he could not remember seeing it anywhere. He would have to search for it.

The first place he ought to

look was the umbrella stand in the hall. Miss Smith left so many things there.

Dodie ran through the cat-flap and into the hall. The umbrella stand was full of the most odd assortment of things.

There was a plastic bag full of

potatoes. There was Miss Smith's handbag, the daily paper, a walking stick and one of Miss Smith's walking-out shoes. Inside the shoe there was Blackie the kitten fast asleep.

But there was no sign of the garden trowel.

Dodie searched all over the house. He could not find the garden trowel. It wasn't in the kitchen; it wasn't in the living room; it wasn't in the bedroom. Dodie decided that it must be in the garden.

Back he went, through the cat-flap and into the garden. First he looked under the lilac tree. The garden trowel was not there. It wasn't among the rose trees. It wasn't among the pansies. Perhaps, thought Dodie, it might be among those pretty yellow flowers he didn't know the name of.

Off he went to have a look. He couldn't see the garden trowel but there was an odd-looking plant that Dodie had never seen before. It was just like one of Miss Smith's cactus plants. Dodie could not imagine what it was doing in the garden, because the cactus plants were always kept in little pots on the big window-sill in the house.

Dodie gave it a poke with his paw, just to make sure that it was as prickly as it looked. It was even more prickly than the other cactus plants in the house. Then much to Dodie's surprise, it moved all by itself and curled up into a prickly ball.

Dodie was very puzzled. He had never seen a cactus plant move before. Those in the house never, ever moved. They just sat in their pots and kept perfectly still.

He sniffed at it to see if it smelt like a cactus plant. No, it didn't smell at all like one. This odd-looking thing must be something else, he thought, though he had no idea exactly what.

Dodie was so surprised by this strange thing that he forgot all about Miss Smith's garden trowel. He went very close to the thing and took another sniff.

Then he heard a very little voice saying, "Please don't keep sniffing at me. I don't like it and it makes me nervous."

Dodie jumped back. He was so surprised to hear this cactus-like thing talking to him.

"Oh," he exclaimed, "I'm sorry if I made you nervous. I

didn't mean to. It's only because I don't know what you are, except that I know you are not a cactus plant because you don't smell like one."

"Of course I'm not a cactus plant," said the tiny voice. "I am a hedgehog. I curl up into a round ball when I'm frightened and then nobody can hurt me because my prickles protect me."

"I don't want to hurt you," answered Dodie. "I didn't know you were here and when I saw you I didn't know what you could possibly be, because I've never seen a hedgehog before."

"Why have you come round here?" asked the hedgehog. "Have you lost something?"

"Well, yes," replied Dodie.

"I was searching for Miss Smith's garden trowel. She forgot where she left it. I don't suppose you've seen it anywhere?" he added hopefully.

"What does it look like?" asked the hedgehog. "I might have seen it lying around."

Dodie tried to explain what a garden trowel looked like. "It's a shiny thing with a handle. People use it to dig holes in the ground."

"Oh, that thing," replied the hedgehog. "I've often wondered what that was. It's over there under the lettuce."

Dodie thanked the hedgehog and ran over to where the lettuce was growing. Hidden under the lettuce was the garden trowel.

He picked it up in his mouth
and took it to Miss Smith. "Oh,
thank you, Dodie. What a
clever little dog you are at
finding things. Now I can dig in
my bedding plants."

Just then Matthew and
Jonathan called to take Dodie
for a walk. Dodie was so
pleased to see them. He wanted
to show them his new friend, the
hedgehog.

Dodie ran over to the pretty yellow flowers he didn't know the name of and barked excitedly. It was too much for the hedgehog. Without saying a word, he curled up into a prickly ball.

Oh dear, thought Dodie. Now I have frightened Mr Hedgehog again. Do uncurl yourself, my friends won't hurt you. They only want to say hello.

Miss Smith, Matthew and Jonathan had all rushed over to the pretty yellow flowers that Dodie didn't know the name of, to see why Dodie was so excited. When Miss Smith saw the hedgehog she was delighted.

"Oh, Dodie, what a clever little dog you are at finding things," she cried. "You have found a hedgehog for the garden."

"Do you want a hedgehog in the garden, Miss Smith?" asked Matthew.

"Most certainly," said Miss Smith. "They eat up all those horrid slugs and all the nasty, creepy-crawly things that nibble away at my cabbage plants. Oh, I do hope he will stay."

Then Miss Smith hurried away into the cottage, and when she came out again she was carrying a saucer full of bread and milk. Carefully she put it on the ground near the pretty yellow flowers that Dodie didn't know the name of.

When Mr Hedgehog smelt

the bread and milk he uncurled
himself at once and started to
eat it all up.

"Well," said Miss Smith,
"perhaps you two boys will help

me with my bedding plants. Oh dear, where is my trowel? I seem to have lost it again."

This time Dodie knew exactly where it was. He took it to Miss Smith. Then he lay down on the lawn again and watched as his friends helped Miss Smith to put in the bedding plants.

He was so pleased to have met Mr Hedgehog, but he did wish that he knew the name of those pretty yellow flowers.